Pearl the Girl

The Fairy Princess of Fun
Book 1

By Laura Hegeman

Illustrated by Jessica Pease

D0109852

Book Design, Formatting and Publishing by
D. D. Scott's
LetLoveGlow Author Services

Indianapolis, Indiana
www.LetLoveGlow.com

To all that sparkle and shine!!

There once was a girl named Pearl.
She shined and she danced and she twirled.

She loved to have fun, and the fun was
never done.

And that's what I know about Pearl.
Well…and a few more wonderful things…

Hi! My name is Pearl. And Fun is my middle name. No, I'm not kidding. My full name is Pearl Fun Pizzazz. For real! Other kids have middle names like Joseph, Elizabeth…you know, ordinary names… but my parents said they knew right away that I was no ordinary girl.

And I love me! Isn't that how it's supposed to be?!

I have this great imagination, but I swear that what I am about to tell you is REALLY true!

Not too long ago, I was taking a walk in the forest behind our house. I'm 8, and I've lived there since I was 0, so I know where all of the paths go. Anyway, this particular day, I chose a path that I had been down thousands of times. I was walking slowly, looking at how tall the trees were and minding my own business when, all of a sudden, I tripped on a root and I fell.

Right before my eyes was the most beautiful fairy you have ever seen. She had a poofy blue dress with gold trim and great looking wings that were super shiny. And get this, she was only about three inches tall.

She looked me in the eye and said, "Hi, Pearl!"

I swear that I almost wet my pants. I couldn't believe that she knew my name. What a surprise! And how exciting, right?!

"Hello," I said.

The beautiful fairy then said, "I have been waiting for you. Follow me."

So, guess what? I did.

We walked around to the trees by the pond and over to a big rock. She flew around me, showing me the way. She was so graceful. I sure wish that I could fly like that, I thought to myself.

"Well, what you think is what you get! Would you like to fly right now?" The fairy replied.

Okay, that was weird because I didn't say a word; I just thought it!

"Listen, fairy, I don't even know your name and you are reading my mind. Do you think you could tell me who you are and how you do that?"

She smiled a sparkling smile and said, "I am Agnes, Fairy of Fun, at your service. I am here to guide you to our land. You are our princess, and we need your help."

I thought that was a real hoot. I mean, I am not a princess. I am about as far from a princess as it gets. But Agnes just continued to smile at me.

"Why do you think your parents named you Pearl Fun Pizzazz? I think if you consider that question you will believe what I say and come with me to save your people."

I became very serious. I considered a land of fairies that needed saving, but I had to admit that I had no idea what a land of fairies looked like, even though I imagined that it was fabulous.

So, I agreed to go wherever Agnes needed to take me as long as I was back in an hour because I had promised my parents that I would be home by then.

Agnes agreed and took hold of my hand. There was a flash, and then millions of tiny stars floated downward and landed all over me. Within seconds, I was only three inches tall, too, and was dressed in a poofy rainbow fairy dress.

I giggled. *Now this is **FUN!***

Immediately, other fairies came over as if they knew I was Princess Pearl. There were shouts of "Here she is!" and "She is real!" and "Princess Pearl, the Princess of Fun, is going to save the day!"

No pressure here! At the same time, though, I knew in my heart that I totally belonged in this land of fairies and that I would do whatever it took to save their land. After all, fun is what it's about. Right?

"Pearl, these are all of your people," Agnes said. "We have waited a long time to meet you and everyone has so much to say but, for now, Stella and Lulu will tell you what is happening."

"In the Land of Fun, all the beautiful shiny stars are the most important. Their twinkling powers our fun, but since the animal came to live in the forest, it is becoming dark and gloomy. The clouds are slowly taking over our land," said Stella, the fairy in the green poofy dress.

"Yes, the stars are not twinkling over us, and the fun we are supposed to bring to others is beginning to fade," said Lulu, dressed all in yellow with sparkling wings.

"Can you help us, Princess Pearl?" Agnes asked.

"I will need all the details. Who is this animal? Where did it come from? How long has it been in the land of fairies? Does it ever come to visit? Has anyone talked to it?" I asked.

All the fairies began talking at once and flying about. It almost sounded like bees flying around looking for the perfect flower. I began to laugh. I laughed so hard I fell over on the ground. The fairies stopped and looked at me. And because this was the Land of Fun, they forgot for a moment that their land was in danger and they, too, fell to the ground laughing. It was quite a sight.

Finally, I straightened myself up and said with a smile, "You are all so beautiful." I sighed, still amazed that I was their princess. "Stella, tell me about the animal."

"No one has seen the dark and gloomy animal that lives in the forest," Stella began. "We only think it is why it's getting so dark and gloomy because every time we hear it, the clouds become thicker. It has been here for seven days. And we are all afraid. No one knows how it got here, what it looks like, and where it came from. Princess Pearl, what should we do?"

"That's easy," I said. "We will have to find the creature and speak to it."

The Land of Fun went completely quiet. No one spoke. It seemed that no one was even breathing.

Finally, Agnes said, "Are you kidding me? This animal is so powerful. It is so dark and gloomy and scary. Pearl, it is not that I doubt your wisdom as our princess, but REALLY?!!! Think about what you are saying!"

All the fairies joined in, whispering things like "Dangerous, and dark and so scary." Finally, I stood on the closest tree stump in my rainbow poofy fairy dress. I stood up as tall as I could and, in a very princess-y voice, I said, "Silence!"

"Trust me," I said and smiled at all of them. "I understand that your very existence is being threatened, and I understand that you are all very frightened. I am only 8, but I am confident that what I say is right. Let's all think from our hearts. Love is the most powerful thing of all. That's what my mom says. I know that we can come to some kind of peaceful understanding with the animal in the forest."

"I am with you, and my heart is with you, too," Stella said. "I'll even go with you to find it!"

"Me too! Me too!" Shouted the other fairies.

"Thank you!" I said, grateful for their love and support. "But I think that Stella and I will go alone. Too many fairies may frighten the animal."

They all agreed to stay behind. Agnes and Lulu had everyone close their eyes and picture the stars shining bright in the sky. They decided to do this until Stella and I returned.

The two of us ventured out toward the forest. This was the first-time I could fly. I couldn't believe how the wind blew through my hair and how easy it was to do. I zipped in and out and around the trees. And I almost forgot that I was on a mission.

As Stella and I got closer to the animal, I could hear its thoughts, and I remembered that Agnes had also heard my thoughts.

And then, there it was, right in front of us…

This creature was as big as a horse, as broad as a cow and get this, it barked like a dog! It had hair sprouting out in different parts of his body, and its head and fur were matted and muddy.

But from where we flew, we thought it looked quite beautiful. We could see and feel what a wonderful animal it really was underneath it all. We knew that on the inside it was filled with rainbow colors.

I listened closer to hear the animal's thoughts.

"I am so lonely. There is no one like me in the whole world. Everyone is afraid of me. I am so sad. Is it because my name is Fred?"

And with every sad and lonely thought I heard coming from the animal, that I now knew was named Fred, the clouds got thicker and thicker. The forest became darker and darker.

Then, from up above, I said as loud as a three-inch princess of fairies can say, "We'll be your friend."

Fred looked up and saw Stella and me flying above his head. He thought maybe he hadn't heard me correctly.

"Oh, but you did hear me right," I said. "I am Pearl, Princess of Fun, and this is my friend Stella. We have come to see what we can do for you. You see, our land has become darker and darker since you have come to live in our forest. The stars are unable to shine through the clouds and, because of that, our fun is being threatened. So, we've come to see if we can help you. We don't want you to be lonely and sad."

Fred blinked once and then he blinked again. He probably couldn't believe that we weren't afraid of him and that we could actually understand what he was thinking.

"It's a fairy thing," Stella said. "We can understand what others are thinking in the forest. I also think you are a wonderful looking animal. I hope we can be friends."

Fred sat and looked at them. And the sky got a tiny bit brighter.

"I have come to the forest because I have been feared by all," he said. "I look different than everyone, and I sound different, too. Creatures run from me and that makes me so sad and lonely."

"We are not afraid of you," I said. "We would like you to come to the Land of Fun and live among us. You are so bright and beautiful. The fairies will be able to understand what you say, and you will be safe and have friends forever. Will you come with us?"

Fred look at Stella and me and, with a smile on his face and tears in his eyes, he began to jump for joy! He shined and danced and twirled. Exactly what one does in the Land of Fun.

All of a sudden, the clouds went away. The stars began to shine and glisten and then millions of them floated down all over Fred.

"I would be honored to come and live in the Land of Fun. Thank you for inviting me, Princess Pearl!" Fred said.

"Follow us, Fred!" I shouted.

And so, Fred ran along the ground and we flew in front of him, showing him the way to his new home.

When we arrived, I said, "We are here with our new friend Fred. He has agreed to come and live with us in The Land of Fun!"

The fairies opened their eyes and looked at the sky. They could see the stars twinkling above and then they saw Fred who was also twinkling brightly. They began fluttering over to him and oohing and aahing!

"Welcome! Welcome home!" They all shouted.

Fred smiled the biggest smile probably possible for a horse-cow-dog and then he once again began to dance and twirl. The fairies all clapped and twirled right with him. It was the beginning of a beautiful friendship.

I took a step back and watched the whole scene. I felt happy and proud of my fairy friends.

Suddenly, Agnes flew up to me.

"Princess Pearl, your hour is almost up! You have to get home!"

I was sad, but happy, all at the same time. I had so much fun. It's not every day you find out that you are the Princess of Fun and that there is a whole land of fairies waiting for you. But, I also knew that it was time to go home and tell my parents about my adventure.

I waved goodbye to my fairy friends and our new friend Fred and promised that I would be back soon to visit. Agnes took me by the hand and away we flew to the exact spot in the forest that we had found one another. I was once again my regular size, and I ran all the way home to tell my family what had happened.

My parents loved hearing about my adventure. And they believed every word because, after all, I was their daughter – Pearl Fun Pizzazz!

Please join Pearl and her fairy friends for a short meditation on my website!

pearlthegirlbooks.com/meditation

Note from The Author

I hope you enjoyed Pearl the Girl. It is the first book in a series to come.

I would love for you to share Pearl with all your friends. AND please leave a short review from wherever you purchased my book! I would really appreciate it!!!

I would love to hear from you directly as well. Feel free to email me at:

laura@pearlthegirlbooks.com

Let me know what you think. I promise to answer you back!

Xo Laura

About The Author

Laura Hegeman is a lifelong storyteller. She believes in focusing on the positives in life and loves to spread fun, happiness, and a little bit of fairy dust wherever she goes. Laura has a master's degree in social work and spent her career working with children. She lives in Golden, CO, has three amazing grown children, and a sweet golden doodle named Chloe.

Books by The Author

The Fairy Princess of Fun
(A Beginning Readers Series)

Pearl the Girl: The Fairy Princess of Fun

Pearl the Girl: Pearl Goes to a Birthday Party –
Coming Soon!

Pearl the Girl: Pearl Goes to School –
Coming Soon!

Made in the USA
Monee, IL
07 April 2021